Es Halloween, querido dragón

It's Halloween,
Dear Dragon

por/by Margaret Hillert

Ilustrado por/Illustrated by Jack Pullan

NORWOOD HOUSE 🏠 PRESS

Querido padre o tutor: Es posible que los libros de esta serie para lectores principiantes les resulten familiares, ya que las versiones originales de los mismos podrían haber formado parte de sus primeras lecturas. Estos textos, cuidadosamente escritos, incluyen palabras de uso frecuente que le proveen al niño la oportunidad de familiarizarse con las más comúnmente usadas en el lenguaje escrito. Estas nuevas versiones han sido actualizadas y las encantadoras ilustraciones son sumamente atractivas para una nueva generación de pequeños lectores.

Primero, léale el cuento al niño, después permita que él lea las palabras con las que esté familiarizado, y pronto podrá leer solito todo el cuento. En cada paso, elogie el esfuerzo del niño para que desarrolle confianza como lector independiente. Hable sobre las ilustraciones y anime al niño a relacionar el cuento con su propia vida.

Al final del cuento, encontrará actividades relacionadas con la lectura que ayudarán a su niño a practicar y fortalecer sus habilidades como lector. Estas actividades, junto con las preguntas de comprensión, se adhieren a los estándares actuales, de manera que la lectura en casa apoyará directamente los objetivos de instrucción en el salón de clase.

Sobre todo, la parte más importante de toda la experiencia de la lectura es ¡divertirse y disfrutarla!

Dear Caregiver: The books in this Beginning-to-Read collection may look somewhat familiar in that the original versions could have been a part of your own early reading experiences. These carefully written texts feature common sight words to provide your child multiple exposures to the words appearing most frequently in written text. These new versions have been updated and the engaging illustrations are highly appealing to a contemporary audience of young readers.

Begin by reading the story to your child, followed by letting him or her read familiar words and soon your child will be able to read the story independently. At each step of the way, be sure to praise your reader's efforts to build his or her confidence as an independent reader. Discuss the pictures and encourage your child to make connections between the story and his or her own life.

At the end of the story, you will find reading activities that will help your child practice and strengthen beginning reading skills. These activities, along with the comprehension questions are aligned to current standards, so reading efforts at home will directly support the instructional goals in the classroom.

Above all, the most important part of the reading experience is to have fun and enjoy it!

Shannon Cannon

Shannon Cannon, Ph.D., Consultora de lectoescritura / Literacy Consultant

Norwood House Press • www.norwoodhousepress.com
Beginning-to-Read ™ is a registered trademark of Norwood House Press.
Illustration and cover design copyright ©2018 by Norwood House Press. All Rights Reserved.

Authorized Bilingual adaptation from the U.S. English language edition, entitled It's Halloween, Dear Dragon by Margaret Hillert. Copyright © 2017 Margaret Hillert. Bilingual adaptation Copyright © 2018 Margaret Hillert. Translated and adapted with permission. All rights reserved. Pearson and Es Halloween, querido dragón are trademarks, in the US and/or other countries, of Pearson Education, Inc. or its affiliates. This publication is protected by copyright, and prior permission to re-use in any way in any format is required by both Norwood House Press and Pearson Education. This book is authorized in the United States for use in schools and public libraries.

LIBRARY OF CONGRESS CATALOGING-IN-PUBLICATION DATA
Names: Hillert, Margaret, author. | Pullan, Jack, illustrator. | Del Risco,
   Eida, translator.
Title: Es Halloween, Querido Dragón = It's Halloween, Dear Dragon / por
   Margaret Hillert ; ilustrado por Jack Pullan ; traducido por Eida Del
   Risco.
Other titles: It's Halloween, Dear Dragon | It is Halloween, Dear Dragon
Description: Chicago, IL : Norwood House Press, [2017] | A beginning-to-read
   book. | Summary: "A boy and his pet dragon enjoy fall activities and
   celebrate Halloween. Spanish/English edition includes reading activities"
   -- Provided by publisher.
Identifiers: LCCN 2016053219 (print) | LCCN 2017014201 (ebook) | ISBN
   9781684040353 (eBook) | ISBN 9781599538365 (library edition : alk. paper)
Subjects: | CYAC: Halloween--Fiction. | Dragons--Fiction. | Spanish language
   materials--Bilingual.
Classification: LCC PZ73 (ebook) | LCC PZ73 .H5572035 2017 (print) | DDC
   [E]--dc23
LC record available at https://lccn.loc.gov/2016053219

Hardcover ISBN: 978-1-59953-836-5   Paperback ISBN: 978-1-68404-022-3

316R—062018
Manufactured in the United States of America in North Mankato, Minnesota.

Mira aquí arriba.
¿Ves lo que yo veo?
Algo rojo.
Algo amarillo.

Look up here.
Do you see what I see?
Something red.
Something yellow.

3

Y mira aquí abajo.
Podemos jugar aquí.
Es divertido.

And look down here.
We can play here.
This is fun.

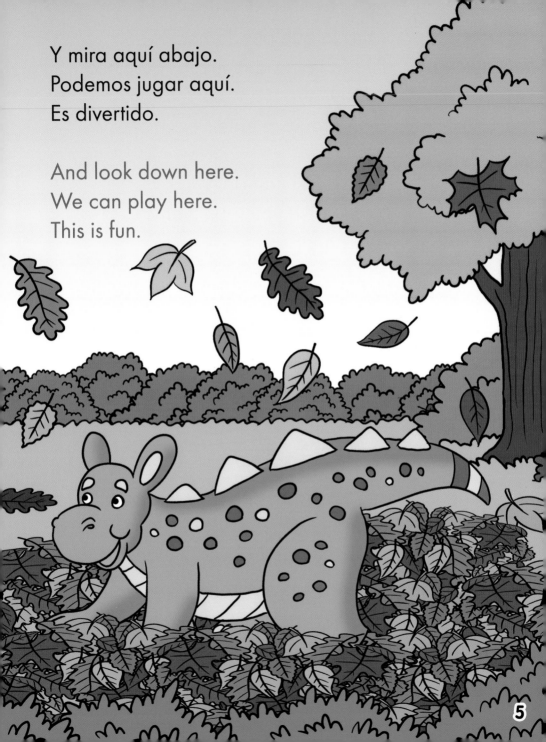

5

Mira lo que puedo hacer.
Puedo hacer que luzcas gracioso.
Ay, ay, ay.
Qué gracioso eres.

See what I can do.
I can make you look funny.
Oh, oh, oh.
Funny, funny you.

Puedo trabajar también.
Trabajar, trabajar y trabajar.
Puedo ayudar a papá.

I can work, too.
Work, work, work.
I can help Father.

Ven aquí.
Ven aquí.
Tú también puedes trabajar.
Puedes ayudar con esto.

Come here.
Come here.
You can work, too.
You can help do this.

Ahora ven conmigo.
Quiero buscar algo.
Tú puedes ayudar.
Corre, corre, corre.

Now come with me.
I want to get something.
You can help.
Run, run, run.

Aquí hay una grande.
Queremos esta.
Y una pequeña también.

Here is a big one.
We want this one.
And a little one, too.

Papá, papá.
Mira lo que tenemos.
¿Puedes ayudarnos a hacer algo?

Father, Father.
Look what we have.
Can you help us make something?

Yo puedo. Yo puedo.
Yo puedo hacerlo.
Mira esta.
¿Te gusta?

I can. I can.
I can do it.
Look at this.
Do you like this?

Y mira esta.
La puedo hacer graciosa.
Se parece a ti.

And look at this one.
I can make it funny.
It looks like you.

Aquí, pequeño.
Sube aquí.
Esto es algo gracioso.
¿Quieres verlo?

Here, little one.
Come up here.
This is something funny.
Do you want to see this?

Mamá, mamá.
¿Puedes hacer algo también?
¿Puedes hacernos algo?

Mother, Mother.
Can you make something, too?
Can you make something for us?

Sí, yo puedo.
Puedo hacer algo bueno.
Les va a gustar.

Yes, I can.
I can make something good.
You will like it.

Mírame.
Mira lo que tengo.
Adivina quién soy.
Adivina, adivina.

Look at me.
See what I have.
Guess who I am.
Guess, guess.

Vamos a entrar aquí.
Será divertido.

We will go in here.
This will be fun.

Tú no.
Tú no.
No, tú tampoco.

Not you.
Not you.
No, you will not do.

23

Aquí.
Eres tú.
Aquí hay algo para ti.
Eres gracioso.

Here.
You are the one.
Here is something for you.
You are funny.

Vaya.
¿Qué veo?
¿Qué tienes ahí?

Oh, my.
What do I see?
What do you have here?

Mira lo que podemos hacer.
Nos vamos.
¡Arriba, arriba y nos alejamos!
Qué buen paseo.

Look what we can do.
Away we go.
Up, up, and away!
What a good ride.

Tú estás conmigo.
Y yo estoy contigo.
Ay, qué Halloween tan feliz,
querido dragón.

Here you are with me.
And here I am with you.
Oh, what a happy Halloween, Dear Dragon.

The following activities support the findings of the National Reading Panel that determined the most effective components for reading instruction are: Phonemic Awareness, Phonics, Vocabulary, Fluency, and Text Comprehension.

Phonemic Awareness: The /h/ sound

Sound Substitution: Say the words on the left to your child. Ask your child to repeat the word, changing the first sound to /**h**/:

pot = hot	book = hook	seal = heal
card = hard	sit = hit	ball = hall
nose = hose	tip = hip	jam = ham

Phonics: The letter Hh

1. Demonstrate how to form the letters **H** and **h** for your child.

2. Have your child practice writing **H** and **h** at least three times each.

3. Ask your child to point to the words in the book that begin with the letter **h**.

4. Write down the following words and ask your child to write the letter **h** in front of them to make a new word:

__air	__and	__eat	__old
__eel	__ear	__is	__ill

5. Read the words aloud. Ask your child to read all the words he or she knows.

Vocabulary: Contractions

1. Explain to your child that sometimes we combine two words to make one shorter word and that these new words are called contractions.

2. Point to the word **It's** on the front cover. Ask your child to name the two words that make **It's**. If your child doesn't know, explain that the word **It's** comes from the two words **it** and **is**.

3. Say the following contractions and ask your child to name the words that make each one:

don't	she's	can't	he'll	we've
I'll	doesn't	you're	isn't	they're

4. Write the following contractions and word pairs on separate pieces of paper.

did not / didn't	we will / we'll	are not / aren't
was not / wasn't	that is / that's	I am / I'm
we are / we're	you will / you'll	did not / didn't
you are / you're	let us / let's	it will / it'll

5. Ask your child to match the word pairs with the contractions they make.

Fluency: Shared Reading

1. Reread the story to your child at least two more times while your child tracks the print by running a finger under the words as they are read. Ask your child to read the words he or she knows with you.

2. Reread the story taking turns, alternating readers between sentences or pages.

Text Comprehension: Discussion Time

1. Ask your child to retell the sequence of events in the story.

2. To check comprehension, ask your child the following questions:

- How did the boy and Dear Dragon help Father?
- What did Father do with the pumpkins?
- How did the boy make the jack-o-lantern look like Dear Dragon?
- Which parts of the story could really happen? Which parts are make believe?
- What do you do to celebrate Halloween?

ACERCA DE LA AUTORA

Margaret Hillert ha ayudado a millones de niños de todo el mundo a aprender a leer independientemente. Fue maestra de primer grado por 34 años y durante esa época empezó a escribir libros con los que sus estudiantes pudieran ganar confianza en la lectura y pudieran, al mismo tiempo, disfrutarla. Ha escrito más de 100 libros para niños que comienzan a leer. De niña, disfrutaba escribiendo poesía y, de adulta, continuó su escritura poética tanto para niños como para adultos.

Photograph by Glenna Washburn

ABOUT THE AUTHOR

Margaret Hillert has helped millions of children all over the world learn to read independently. She was a first grade teacher for 34 years and during that time started writing books that her students could both gain confidence in reading and enjoy. She wrote well over 100 books for children just learning to read. As a child, she enjoyed writing poetry and continued her poetic writings as an adult for both children and adults.

ACERCA DEL ILUSTRADOR

Jack Pullan, ilustrador talentoso y creativo, es graduado de William Jewell College. También ha estudiado informalmente en la Universidad de Oxford y en el Instituto de Arte de Kansas City. Sus mentores han sido los renombrados acuarelistas Jim Hamil y Bill Amend. La obra de Jack ha adornado las páginas de numerosos y placenteros libros para niños, diversos materiales educativos y tiras cómicas, así como también muchas tarjetas de felicitación. Jack reside actualmente en Kansas.

ABOUT THE ILLUSTRATOR

A talented and creative illustrator, Jack Pullan, is a graduate of William Jewell College. He has also studied informally at Oxford University and the Kansas City Art Institute. He was mentored by the renowned watercolor artists, Jim Hamil and Bill Amend. Jack's work has graced the pages of many enjoyable children's books, various educational materials, cartoon strips, as well as many greeting cards. Jack currently resides in Kansas.